SUMMER IN SORRENTO

MELISSA HILL

Original published by Simon & Schuster, UK, 2014
This edition, copyright Little Blue Books, 2018

The right of Melissa Hill to be identified as the Author of the Work has been asserted by her in accordance with the Copyright, Designs and Patents Act 1988.

All rights reserved. No part of this publication may be reproduced, stored in a retrieval system, or transmitted, in any form or by any means without the prior written permission of the author. You must not circulate this book in any format.

All characters in this publication are fictitious and any resemblance to real persons, living or dead is purely coincidental.

SUMMER IN SORRENTO

CHAPTER 1

A balmy breeze floated through the open kitchen window and tickled the back of Maia's neck as she stood at the sink washing lemons she'd just plucked from fruit trees languishing in full sunshine at the side of her farmhouse.

Taking a deep breath, she closed her eyes and allowed her senses to take it all in.

She smelled the azaleas that had just come to life outside her window—their fragrance mixed with the scent of saltwater spray floating up distantly from the Bay of Naples below.

Opening her eyes, the view that her husband Jim had loved so much welcomed her, and she dropped the lemon she had been holding in a colander, allowing herself a momentary respite to simply 'be.'

Glancing down at the ring on her left hand, she used the fingers of her right to twirl it longingly, remembering the magical day that Jim had placed it there.

"I hope you can see what I see right now, love," she whispered to the air—her Irish accent peppering her words.

She imagined that Jim was standing next to her, remembering how much he loved to simply take in the view of Mt. Vesuvius and the gorgeous expanse of the bay spread before them.

A sense of sadness as well as peace washed over her all at once, and she had the overwhelming sense that she was quite close to heaven at that particular moment—safe inside the nineteenth century farmhouse on a steep Sorrento hillside that she and her husband had bought upon his retirement three years before.

Smiling sadly, she gathered up the lemons. "And honestly my love," she said to the air, "I hope that you like what I've been doing with the place."

Maia glanced around the kitchen that she - along with the help of some local workmen - had just finished renovating the week before. Working on introducing the nineteenth century structure to the twenty-first century had been a labor of love at the best, and a heartbreaking endeavour at worst. She also knew without a doubt that the entire process would have been much easier with Jim around.

But fate sometimes had other plans.

The house, aptly named Villa Azalea, had been Jim's dream—and his one passion outside of love for his wife—right until the end. And as much as Maia missed her husband, she knew that she couldn't blame the house for his heart attack.

She stacked the freshly picked lemons on a ceramic bowl she had bought during a recent trip to Naples, and placed the lot in the center of the rustic oak kitchen table they'd brought from Dublin when they moved to Italy.

"Though I suppose I can definitely blame this place for some of my money problems..." she mused aloud, ruefully looking around the space, and quickly calculating how much of their savings had been spent on each part of the renovation.

Fresh paint, twenty euro. New windows, three hundred euro. Butchers block countertops, priceless, she thought to herself.

Now just to figure out a way to pay off the credit card bills...

As if providing an answer to her train of thought, Maia suddenly heard a car pull up outside the house. The sound of an engine idling lingered a little, before stopping altogether.

She smiled as she walked out the back door and wound her way down the dirt path that led to the main road sweeping past where the house was perched.

Trotting through the lemon trees that bordered the walkway, she raised a hand to shield her eyes as she made her way out of the shade and into the brilliant Italian sunshine.

There, she found an older couple; obviously tourists, peering at the mason jars full of olives that she had so carefully cleaned and canned the night before—displaying them for sale inside a small wooden stand that her neighbor

Giorgio, had built for her at the end of last winter.

"*Buongiorno!*" she called out happily. "*Grazie per l'arresto. Posso aiutarla?*" Thanks for stopping. Can I help you?

The man, who appeared to be in his mid-sixties, looked at his wife before stating in stilted Italian, "*Salve. Si. Hai belle olive. I limoni sono piuttosto troppo. Posso acquistare un pesce?*" Hi. Yes. You have beautiful olives. Lemons are pretty too. Can I buy a fish?

"I'm afraid I don't have any fish to sell. But I can certainly help with the lemons and olives," Maia laughed. "I can also speak English if it's easier," she asked, watching relief immediately flood the man's face.

"Oh, er, yes. Fantastic. Yes, English is better as we are - British, that is. Just here on holiday," said the man.

"Your accent," his companion called out. "Is it Irish?"

Maia nodded an affirmation. "I am indeed Irish. Welcome to Sorrento. You picked a beautiful part of the world to visit. Is it your first time?" she inquired.

"To Amalfi Coast, yes. Italy, no," said the

woman, walking forward to offer her hand to Maia. "Kent and Cora Beauchamp. It's nice to meet you."

"Maia Connolly, and a pleasure."

"Do you live here?" Kent asked.

"I have for three years now," she stated simply.

"Well, there are worse places," he laughed. "And you can't beat this weather, eh? We left London two days ago in drizzle and cold. Nothing beats an Italian summer."

"Indeed," Maia smiled.

Cora held up two jars of olives and a bag containing five or six lemons. "*Quanto?*" she asked in Italian. How much?

Maia did the math in her head. "Ten euro, please."

Kent reached into his pocket and extracted a note. "Thank you kindly." He shot a glance at the house behind Maia. "And you live here alone? Do you feel safe? A woman in a foreign country?"

Knowing that this line of questioning usually came eventually, she nodded and slipped the tenner in her pocket.

"Quite safe. And yes, I do live alone. You see

my husband passed away two years ago. This was his dream. To buy an Italian farmhouse, restore it and make it our own. Unfortunately Jim had a bad heart."

Cora put a dramatic hand to her mouth, as if to cover up her shock. "Oh, you poor thing. And now you are left here all alone?"

Maia smiled. "Ah, well, there are worse places," she nodded ruefully at Kent, having stolen his words from the moment previous.

She exchanged pleasantries for a few more minutes with the couple, before bidding them farewell and providing directions for driving to the ruins of Pompeii, about a half hour or so away.

Waving goodbye as they got in their rented Fiat and drove down the winding hill that was essentially her front yard, Maia turned her attention back to the house. She made her way back up the pathway, only to find Camilla, the twenty-two year old local girl who helped her with household chores, standing in the doorway.

"Well?" the Italian said in heavily accented English, hands on her hips. Accusation was thick in her voice.

"Well what?" Maia said innocently. "They wanted to buy some fruit and olives. Ten euro." She took the money out of her pocket and waved it in Camilla's face before walking past her and back into the house. There, she placed the bill in a jar on the kitchen counter, where she typically kept the money she made from the roadside stand until heading to the bank in Naples once a week.

"You know what I mean," chastised Camilla. "Did you tell them you have rooms to rent? They looked like tourists."

Maia turned around to face the young woman, leaning against the counter. "Yes, they were tourists. British. But I'm fairly sure they already have somewhere to stay."

Camilla tisked. "They might have somewhere to stay *right now*, but if they don't know it exists, how will they know to return to this place, and stay *here*? Sorry my friend, but you aren't going to be able to keep this place going just by selling lemons and olives."

Maia frowned. It was true, she knew that. But she also knew that the house wasn't ready yet to house visitors.

"I just don't think it's up to scratch…"

But the young woman was already shaking her head.

"You have a working kitchen. You have several bedrooms. You have indoor plumbing. You are set on a beautiful cliffside in Sorrento." Camilla motioned to the scenery that lay beyond the kitchen window, as if Maia had forgotten where she was. "And you have friends. People like me and Giorgio, to help you. What else do you need?"

Grimacing, Maia couldn't deny the truth in her words. She had been trying to figure out how to make money off the investment that she and Jim had made in the farmhouse—and the fact was she needed money more than ever now if she was going to keep this place—and not have to return to Ireland and to her work as a graphic designer.

Admittedly, living with the spirit of Jim on a hillside in Italy was a more attractive idea. But this idyllic dream unfortunately didn't pay for itself. And Maia was almost out of savings.

"Maybe you're right, Camilla," she began thoughtfully.

"Of course I'm right," the other woman tisked afresh. "But how will you fill up rooms and find guests if you keep your mouth shut when people drive by and stop? *This* is how I know you have no Italian blood. If I were you, I would be shouting the news from the rooftops."

She stared Maia down, challenging her.

But thankfully, Maia already had an answer to Camilla's conundrum, one which thankfully didn't involve shouting.

"So what do you think?" she asked a few days later, turning her laptop screen around to face the other woman.

Camilla, who had been standing at the kitchen counter arranging freshly-picked azaleas in a glass vase, turned in Maia's direction and approached the wooden table that her friend was sitting at.

Pulling a chair out and placing herself in it, she leaned in close and examined what Maia offered on her screen.

"It's … how do you say it? *Semplice*," she commented, looking unimpressed.

Maia smiled. "Simple? Yes, I would say it is. But I'm not designing a website for the Ritz

Hotel after all. We're a private guesthouse. Or at least intending to be. Not exactly a multi-national conglomerate," she remarked watching Camilla's face fall.

"You are thinking too small," her friend scolded, standing up again and returning to her place at the counter.

"I'm thinking realistically. I've put up pictures that show the house honestly. They are beautiful pictures mind you, but I also have to express that the farmhouse isn't finished yet. That yes, there are civilised comfortable areas, but if I want to make a long-term go of actually establishing a business—and not just getting bad reviews on TripAdvisor, then I need to be upfront from the start. *L'onestà è la miglio politica.*"

Camilla smiled and placed the bouquet of flowers in the middle of the kitchen table. "Honesty is the best policy?"

Maia nodded. "It truly is. Okay, the site is live. Villa Azalea is now open for business. Let's see what, if *anything*, we get."

CHAPTER 2

If Maia was being honest with herself, she wasn't expecting to suddenly be an overnight success in the hospitality industry—in fact, she was still wrapping her head around the idea of hosting strangers in her home.

She'd been watching the website nervously all week, so much so that she even worried that her website design skills were more than a little rusty.

First, she decided to Google herself in order to make sure the website did show up —and then, certain that the gods were working against her somehow, called Giorgio her neighbour and friend who lived just down the road, and asked him to do the same.

She was relieved when he confirmed that yes, he had found Villa Azalea's website.

Feeling that she had accomplished something at least, though she wouldn't likely need to worry about bookings for some time, she opened a bottle of Chianti, poured herself a glass and headed to the back patio overlooking the Bay, with the intent to sit and watch the sunset over the clear, crystal blue waters of the Mediterranean.

Settling back in a wooden deck chair that Jim had built when they first moved to Italy, Maia thought back over the journey that had brought her to where she was today. Her husband had said that it was necessary to enjoy this view before all other things, including a finished or renovated house.

The breeze ruffled the branches of the surrounding lemon trees, and she felt an instant wave of calm wash over her. It was always here, in this spot, drinking wine and simply relaxing, where she felt closest to Jim.

She'd been truly devastated when he died—had never expected to be a widow in her mid-forties, and the idea of being alone in a foreign country without the benefit of family or an extensive network of friends had almost set her running back to Ireland.

But Maia had realised something.

Italy, and the experience that she and Jim had in this country together, albeit a short one, had been uniquely theirs.

Her life in Ireland had other dynamics at play—and she worried that if she went back, she risked losing the part of Jim—that essence—that had made him so happy in the days before his heart attack.

Her sister, Joyce in Dublin had told her that by staying in Italy she was pursuing an impossible dream, and living in the past. But Maia disagreed—and instead committed herself to living the reality that Jim dreamed of, but had sadly missed out on.

Now, she breathed the delicious citrus scent floating around her nose, and looked out over the horizon. She watched as an ocean liner made its way steadily out of the Bay, and toward the open sea.

"Floating hotels Jim, that's what you always

called them wasn't it?" Maia smiled, talking to the air.

She chuckled at the memory; he could never understand how tourists believed that this was 'visiting' another country, taking a boat from place to place, disembarking to hit up the souvenir stalls in order to buy a fridge magnet so that they could tell people at home that they had 'seen' Naples or 'been to' Sorrento.

"Do you think I'm likely to get visitors like that here?" she asked the sky, only to be greeted by silence. She took a sip of her wine and paused for a moment to close her eyes and relish the fragrant bouquet that tickled her tongue. "No," she whispered. "It's not likely I'd get cruise-goers, not if they want to stay overnight. But I wonder who *will* visit me."

She opened her eyes and looked back over the Bay, then stood up and wandered toward the hillside, feeling a sense of wonder and history all at once.

"It really is a magical place," she sighed. "You were right about that. How many people through the ages have stood in this spot, and seen this same view?"

Maia had a tremendous sense of longing for her late husband and wished so desperately that she would feel Jim walk up behind her right at that moment, and wrap his arms around her. She tilted her head up to feel the last rays of the sun on her face and focused on remembering what it felt like when Jim kissed her throat, making his way lazily up to find her lips.

"Oh I hope I'm doing the right thing honey. I really do. I know you loved this place, and I want to make it work, so I can stay here," Maia whispered to the Italian sunset. Suddenly feeling desperate, and totally worried that she didn't have the business ability to pull off an Italian villa-style guesthouse, nor the necessary skills needed to entertain groups of people and make them feel like they were in their home away from home, she added urgently, "Jim, maybe give me a sign? If I'm doing what I should be doing—opening our place up to visitors—let me know."

She sucked in her breath, as if waiting for a bolt of lightning to crisscross the pale pink sky, but nothing came. Then Maia bit her lip and shook her head, feeling chagrined at her own silliness when suddenly Camilla's voice trilled from the house.

"Maia! Maia! P*resto!*" Come quick!

A moment later, the Italian girl tore from the house, skirt fluttering behind her. When she came into view, her face was flushed with excitement; her tanned cheeks a burst of rosy color.

"Camilla? What is it? What's happened?" Maia asked, immediately worrying there was a disaster of some sort—something was on fire, or a pipe had burst. "What's the emergency?" She thought of her bank account and the reserve she had on hand to cope with whatever tragedy had befallen them.

Or rather, lack thereof. Panic engulfed her.

But Camilla was shaking her head. "*Nessuna emergenza!*" No emergency. "It's the website. I was on your computer. It's official! We have our first booking!"

A wave of relief flooded Maia's body. There was no emergency. Then tears pricked at her eyes and she gave a wistful smile.

But she did get a sign.

Our first booking. Thank you, my darling.

CHAPTER 3

A week later, working with Camilla to fluff pillows and make beds in the guest rooms, Maia brushed a lock of errant hair out of her face and wiped a bead of sweat as it formed on her brow.

"I suppose this is what you might call trial by fire," she said as she turned to the window and threw it open to welcome in the Mediterranean breeze. "When did Giorgio say he was going to come up and take a look at the air conditioning unit? Of course it's our luck that it decides to banjax itself at just the right time…" she fretted, feeling a wave of panic grow in her stomach.

But Camilla simply waved a hand. "It's

practically a new unit. Besides the air conditioning—it's no big thing. Not with scenery around us like this." She motioned to the window, as if the view of Mt. Vesuvius would make up for the fact that the greater Naples area was suddenly having one of the hottest Junes on record—and that the house felt every bit the oven that it was.

Maia smiled knowingly, certain that most tourists valued air conditioning above all things. "I suppose we will just have to deal with it. But I feel it's rather a cruel joke."

Camilla looked at her friend, puzzled. "So the visitors will find it funny?" she asked. "Well, *that's* good."

But before Maia could explain her intent, she heard a car pull up outside, its wheels grinding against the gravel of the drive before it came to a stop.

"Oh that must be Giorgio—thank goodness," said Maia, finalising laying out a set of bath towels in the room and smoothing back her hair. "Hopefully he can make this place a few degrees cooler—this is what it must feel like *inside* Mt. Vesuvius."

She left the room as Camilla called out.

"How silly you are—the volcano, it's not active you know."

Shaking her head, Maia stifled a laugh. *No, her friend definitely didn't get irony.*

Going through the kitchen and to the exterior door with purpose, Maia readied herself to call a greeting to Giorgio, when she was suddenly met with a car that she had never seen before and a person who she didn't know, getting out of it.

Oh blast it, a guest—and they're early!

Since receiving her first booking the week before, Maia had been shocked to find herself with subsequent reservations - enough for a soon-to-be full house.

Indeed it felt as if by the time one reservation had come in, she just as quickly had three —a booking for each guest room—and she made the quick decision to ensure that the website was updated with the announcement that they were fully booked for the time being.

Nothing like jumping in feet first, she pondered. Though what she'd first thought was a sign from Jim that she was doing the right thing had quickly morphed into her wondering if he was playing some sort of practical joke on her from the ether.

That would be just his style.

Putting a smile on her face, she opened the door and stepped into the Italian sunshine just as the young man - apparently her first guest - closed the door of his Mercedes, an obvious rental by the sticker in its window, and opened the boot to extract his bag.

Quickly thinking back through the reservations she had received, Maia realised that this must be Jacob Bellafonte. The New Yorker. He was due to arrive today, but not until the evening.

"*Buongiorno!*" she called out. "*Benvenuto!* Good day! Welcome!"

The man looked quickly at the house and Maia and gave a quick nod.

"Hey there," he said quickly. "Jacob Bellafonte. You must be Maia." He crossed the distance between them in five long strides and extended his hand. "Sorry I'm early. My flight got in ahead of schedule. We must have had a good tailwind from Manhattan. I hope that's not a problem."

Maia shook his hand as she noticed his strong New York accent and she wondered what brought him to Italy.

Looking to be in his mid-thirties, he was handsome and dressed in a dark suit, which she immediately recognised as a custom Armani. He had a watch with a large face on his wrist—the diamond inlay showed it was a Movado—and Maia was sure that the shoes were also Italian—Gucci perhaps? All in all, Jacob looked successful and moneyed—and she immediately wondered why he had opted to stay here.

Not that her place wasn't lovely of course, but she had priced it rather cheaply because it was unfinished, and the man in front of her looked better suited for one of Naples five-star luxury hotels.

"I am. Maia, that is," she replied with what she hoped was an inviting smile. "And no, it's not a problem. So lovely to have you with us, Jacob. Is that your only bag? Here let me get that for you." She briefly remembered the episode of *Downton Abbey* she had been watching the night before and wondered if

Carson, the fictional head butler, would approve of her behavior.

But Jacob shook his head. "I can manage. It's no problem. You're English then?"

"No but close, Irish. And it's easy to tell that you're American. I mean that in a good way, of course," she grinned. "Please come inside."

Maia graciously led the way into the kitchen, where they found Camilla, who immediately straightened at the sight of the attractive young man with dark good looks. It was clear that Jacob was definitely her type, as much by the younger woman's hungry expression as the way she immediately puffed out her chest, making sure her impressive assets were introduced first.

Oh good Lord, Maia thought, she's like a strutting peacock. "Camilla, meet Jacob Bellafonte, our first guest. Jacob this is Camilla di Mariano Filipepi—my er, helper." Maia could hazard a guess as to exactly what Camilla wanted to help this particular guest with.

"*Ciao, siete I benvenuti,*" her friend purred batting her eyelashes seductively. Hello, you are *most* welcome. Maia heard the inflection of her words.

Jacob turned and looked at Maia. "Is it okay if we speak English? I mean, I hate to be that guy but..."

"Of course."

"Yes, that is fine, my English is wonderful too," smiled Camilla.

Jacob gave a weak grimace and shifted from one foot to the other. "I mean it's not like I don't speak Italian, I was born here," he added quickly. "But I just prefer not to."

Maia furrowed her brow. Seemed like a strange thing to visit Italy if you didn't like to speak Italian – and could.

"I'm assuming you are here on business then?" She again looked him up and down—the suit screamed business traveller, but again his choice of lodging contradicted that assumption.

"Not quite," Jacob shrugged. "It's family. My father lives here—in Naples. And well, to be frank, he's dying. So that's why I am here." Maia realised at once that his voice lacked both sympathy and empathy.

But Camilla didn't catch this, as she practically lunged forward—her actions were so dramatic she belonged in a Fellini flick.

"Oh no how tragic, I'm so sorry. This must be so difficult for you. Are you close to him, your father?"

A cloud passed over Jacob's face and he answered simply, "No. Which is why I'm staying here." He turned to look at Maia. "If you don't mind, could I be shown to my room? It's been a long night, getting here, and I would like to get cleaned up."

Maia rushed forward immediately, mortified that she hadn't thought to bring him to the room first thing.

Clearly she had a lot to learn…

"Of course, if you would just follow me this way—we'll get you all set up. Please forgive the heat; our AC unit is on the blink, but it will be taken of shortly."

Her curiosity piqued by Jacob's ready dismissal of his family situation, Maia gave Camilla a glare that conveyed caution, and quickly changed the topic.

Still she (and indeed Camilla) needed to remember that Villa Azalea was a guesthouse, not a therapy clinic, and that her guests' reasons for being here would of course be varied.

But more to the point, absolutely none of her business.

CHAPTER 4

"Is he settled in his room?" Camilla inquired as Maia re-entered the kitchen, fresh from making sure that Jacob had all required amenities.

Wiping her hands nervously on her skirt, Maia shrugged, "I suppose in a manner of speaking—he has a bed to sleep in, fresh bath towels and a roof over his head."

"But did you hear him? His family lives close by—and his father is dying. Clearly, something isn't right between them, otherwise, why on *earth* would he stay here?" Camilla glanced in the direction of Jacob's room, a forlorn look on her tanned face. "So sad. I can't imagine not being close to my family, especially my papa. Maybe we should ask him?"

Maia's eyes widened. She shook her head.

"No, no that's very forward Camilla. We shouldn't be that direct with a stranger, regardless that he is staying in this house. Not my business." Maia then shot a warning glance at her. "Or *yours* for that matter."

The young woman shrugged and faced toward the kitchen window. She turned on the tap and began filling a pot with water, in an effort to begin making pasta noodles for whatever lunch she had planned. Instinctively Maia's stomach grumbled. Camilla was an excellent cook.

"I suppose that is the difference with Italians. We say whatever we are thinking. No holding back. Probably why we have such low blood pressure, too. If we are angry, everyone knows it. Feeling happy, well, all those around us know it too. There are no secrets in my family," she smiled, "we always say what we are thinking."

Maia laughed. "Yes, I'd kinda gathered that." Turning toward a wine rack that she kept on the counter, she grabbed a bottle of Sangiovese.

"What do you think? Too early in the day? My nerves are a bit frazzled from welcoming our first guest."

"It's never too early in the day to drink in Italy," scoffed Camilla. "Please, you should know that by now."

The pair opened the bottle and savored a glass while Camilla cooked. Smells wafted from the stove as finely scented basil and garlic were added to a stewed tomato base. They swirled around Maia's head, and she had a brief flashback of sitting there at the kitchen table while Jim filled Camilla's role—cooking succulent Italian dishes, just for the two of them. She had a sudden pang of longing, spurring her to finish her glass and pour another.

"Life's too short," sighed Maia. She was speaking to herself more than anything, but Camilla answered.

"For what?" she asked, turning briefly from the stove. "Fighting with your family?"

Maia gave a meek shrug. "Yes. That. And other things, too."

Thankfully, her melancholy was broken by the fact that Camilla was finished cooking lunch and her attention was turned to the plate of delicious looking pasta that was placed in front of her.

"Oh Camilla, you have outdone yourself, once again, I hope you know that I would be twenty pounds lighter if it weren't for you."

Camilla smiled happily. "Food is the flavor of life. Now you stay put. I will go ask our guest if he wants to join us."

Happy to do as she was told, Maia dug in, working her hardest to think happy thoughts instead of the mournful bouts that sometimes entered her subconscious.

She couldn't deny that she missed Jim—horribly so—but she also knew that she had a life to live, and that he would not be pleased if she wrapped herself and her brain in a constant state of widow's weeds, dwelling only on the life that she had before everything changed.

Jim would always want her to *live*.

Feeling contentment overcome her now, she took another sip of wine as Camilla reentered the kitchen, this time with a somewhat dour look on her face. Immediately, Maia knew what had happened.

"Let me guess," she smirked, "he's not hungry."

Camilla sat down across the table from her with a definitive clatter. "Who is not hungry in Italy?" It was less of a question that an accusation, Maia thought. "*Di tutte le cose stupide...*" her friend muttered.

"Now now, it's not stupid. He's just not hungry. Let the guy get settled in before you try seducing him with your food."

Camilla narrowed her eyes at Maia. "Fine. When he is hungry, I will just make him a new dish. He cannot escape me for long."

Maia giggled. She had the immediate mental picture of Camilla standing over a cauldron, brewing a love potion that came in the form of fresh pasta and large amounts of Italian vino. However, the picture was interrupted by the sound of a small voice echoing from the doorway beyond where they sat.

"Um, excuse me. *Perdonatemi?*" Pardon me. "I'm wondering if I am in the right place?" said a properly accented British voice.

CHAPTER 5

Startled, Camilla and Maia both turned to find a young woman in her mid-twenties, standing in the entryway.

She had her blonde hair pulled back into a severe chignon and a pair of dark sunglasses shielded her eyes, even though she was now practically indoors. She wore a pink sundress and gold sandals and would have looked perfectly at home as a tourist in the brilliant Italian landscape, but lines of worry that etched her forehead and around her mouth gave her away.

Tension radiated from her body and Maia immediately felt the slight buzz she had been experiencing from the wine she'd been drinking, evaporate.

"It depends on where you are supposed to be," she smiled kindly, getting up from the table. "I'm Maia. And this is Camilla. And you are?"

"Amelia Crawley. I made a reservation for this guesthouse online. Just two days ago. This is a guesthouse, Villa Azalea?"

Maia nodded. "You're in the right place. And yes, we were expecting you Amelia. Did you find us okay?"

Amelia stole a glance around the kitchen, as if trying to determine if her choice of lodging had been a wise one. Her face practically screamed the words, "Stranger danger."

"Yes, it was easy. I was so glad you had rooms available. My trip was a bit … last minute. Everything in the area was booked … well except one place, and I didn't want to stay there because … just, because."

Maia and Camilla exchanged a glance, immediately wondering what Amelia meant. After Jacob's introduction, they suddenly felt on high alert about hidden messages in their guests' words.

"So are you in Sorrento on holiday?"

Amelia shook her head sadly. "Definitely *not* a holiday. My ... um friend, is getting married. On Saturday. I just decided to come at the last minute."

"How nice," Camilla crooned. "Weddings are so lovely. Especially in this area and at this time of year. What a wonderful time you will have."

Shrugging, Amelia offered a meek smile. The young woman once again looked around the kitchen, her eyes finally settling on the half-eaten meal that her hosts had obviously just been sharing. "Oh I apologise, I seem to have interrupted your lunch."

But Maia jumped forward. "No, of course not. You didn't interrupt. And really, would you like to join us? We have plenty of food and Camilla is an excellent cook. Please sit down, relax, have a glass of wine."

Amelia shifted from one foot to the next and she looked poised to decline the invitation, but then her stomach gave her away. A tiny but polite grumble was heard and she blushed.

"It has been a long morning. I hate airplane

food, and Gatwick is such a nightmare… All right then."

Quickly fetching another pasta bowl and wine glass, Maia made a home for Amelia at the table. Once seated, the slight-looking English girl had no trouble tucking into her dish of pasta.

"This is really wonderful. Thank you."

Camilla beamed with pleasure. There was no quicker way to win her over than by complimenting her cooking.

"So where is the wedding?" Maia asked with a smile, eager to engage their new guest.

But Amelia kept her head down, focused on her dish. Finally she spoke.

"Um, down the coast somewhere. I'd have to look at the details on the invite," she offered vaguely

"Your friends must be so happy that you made the journey here—to come to their wedding. Have you and the bride been friends for a long time?" Camilla pressed.

Suddenly, Amelia looked up and met Camilla's eyes directly. "No, I'm not friends with the bride."

Which insinuated that she was friends with

the groom. Opening her mouth to inquire more, Maia all of a sudden noticed the stony look on Amelia's young face—there was pain there that was far more advanced than her years, and she felt at a loss for words.

Closing her mouth and reaching out to grab her wine glass, she caught the look of relief that washed across Amelia's face—as if she was pleased that the questions had ended.

Taking a sip of the fragrant liquid, Maia pondered all that occurred that morning.

It seemed that they had more than one mysterious houseguest on their hands…

CHAPTER 6

Later that afternoon, Maia and Camilla sat outside fanning themselves, hoping to catch a breeze as it lifted off the Bay.

They were each trying desperately to avoid the hotbox that the inside of the house had become without air conditioning when Giorgio, the handyman neighbour, pulled up in his battered utility truck.

"Oh thank the Lord," Maia exclaimed, casting a quick glance at the house. "I love Giorgio but sometimes he moves as slow as molasses in January."

Camilla furrowed her brow as she attempted to understand the colloquialism. "Molasses in…"

"Never mind," she smiled, not wanting to go into the nuances with her Italian friend. "It's just great that he's here, and before the last guests arrive too. I just don't understand how Amelia has been able to put up with the heat inside all afternoon."

After lunch, Amelia had retired to her room —commenting that she was going to have a nap.

Jacob the New Yorker, on the other hand had emerged from his room as Camilla and Maia cleaned up after lunch. He took a quick look around and having successfully evaded Camilla's attempts to cook him a meal, mumbled something about the hospital in Naples before getting into his car and driving off.

Maia felt the mystery of her guests thicken with every interaction, while Camilla simply mourned the lost opportunity of wooing Jacob with her culinary skills.

Returning her attention to the matter of the air conditioning and Giorgio, who was gathering a variety of tools from his truck, Maia muttered, "I just hope this isn't too expensive."

She was weary of writing cheques and

paying bills—she needed just a brief respite from the stress—and to make a bit of progress in paying back her investment.

"Ciao!" Giorgio called as he walked up the path to the house. *"Ho sentito dire che è un po 'una calda nella vostra casa."* I hear it's a bit hot in your house.

That's the understatement of the year, Maia thought ruefully, casting a glance at Mt. Vesuvius in the distance.

"Just a bit," she answered. "I'm hoping you can fix it quickly—I am close to having a house full of guests and I don't want to put anyone through any more unnecessary discomfort."

Giorgio shook his head with a smile.

"You know in Italy we have survived for centuries without the benefit of cool air—we have never worried so much about air conditioning. All through the ages, we have survived."

Maia suppressed a grin—she truly loved Giorgio, and was appreciative of everything he did for her, usually at a discount, but just then she didn't need a history lesson on the superiority of the Italian people compared to other apparently 'lesser' ethnicities.

"Yes yes, I know Giorgio—let's talk Italian history later. Now, come inside the house." She extended a hand to her friend as if to guide him to where he needed to be when she heard another car pull up.

Realising that it couldn't be Jacob returning so soon, Maia knew that her wish to have the AC fixed before her last guests arrived had been an empty thought—they were already here.

Thinking back quickly to the other reservation – this one for a couple - she recalled the names—Parish. They were also Americans, from Florida and apparently visiting Italy for their wedding anniversary.

"Camilla can you take Giorgio into the house? Some more guests just arrived."

FOLLOWING HER INSTRUCTIONS, the Italian pair disappeared into the house, leaving Maia to once again put a welcoming smile on her face as she worked to suppress the stress and nervousness.

"Hello!" she called out, deciding this time to forego the Italian welcome given that they were American and probably more comfortable with English. "You must be the Parishes?"

Maia headed down the walk to where the couple stood. Taking in their appearance, she immediately decided that they had to be in their late forties, probably closer to her in age than either Amelia or Jacob. She wondered what wedding anniversary they were celebrating.

"Hi," said Lori, "we are - the Parishes that is. And you must be Maia. We are so happy you had a vacancy—this place looks perfect."

Lori had bright red hair and Maia knew right off the bat that she was a natural redhead, as much because of her pale ivory skin dotted with freckles, as the fact that the highlights in her hair simply could not be bought in a salon.

Maia smiled at the compliment. "Well, thank you for that, but in the interests of full disclosure, I just want to warn you that our air conditioning is broken at the moment. It's a new unit though and we do have someone working on it currently. I have no doubt we will have cooler air inside shortly."

With her comment Hal, the husband of the pair, perked up. "I know something about air conditioning. For my engineering degree I worked for a heating and air company in Orlando. I can go help if you like."

Maia shook her head, touched.

"Oh, I appreciate it. But you're on holiday! You don't need to do that. Besides, my handyman, Giorgio; he's the one who installed it. I'm sure he can manage."

Lori looked to her husband, clearly in agreement with what Maia was saying. "Come on honey, she's right, it's our vacation. You don't need to go mess with the AC, they'll get it fixed."

But Hal was shaking his head. "No really, I don't mind. Point me in the right direction. What did you say his name was? Giorgio?" He pronounced it "Georgie-O" without the necessary Italian accent.

"Um," Maia said, looking nervously between the pair, and feeling immediately worried when she saw the happy expression that had been on Lori's face disappear. "I mean, yes, Giorgio is his name, but honestly he has it covered. You shouldn't feel the need to do this — you are a guest after all."

But her words had obviously fallen on deaf

ears. At that moment, Giorgio emerged from the house, apparently to fetch another tool from his truck, and Hal honed in. Seemed he knew he was the AC repair guy by sight alone.

"Hey man," Hal called. "You fixing the AC? Need an extra pair of hands? I know what I'm doing in that department."

Giorgio, who had pulled a rag from his back pocket to wipe grease off his hands, cast a curious, albeit confused look at Maia. For a moment, she just hoped that her friend would pretend to not understand English in an effort to deflect Hal's help—but no such luck.

"Yes. I am trying to fix it now, but - "

However Hal didn't allow Giorgio to offer any protest.

He'd already dropped the bag that he was holding on the ground and was walking forward, ready to help.

"Great. I used to work in heating and cooling—a long time ago, but I know my way around a repair, you know? So what are you dealing with? How many BTUs? Is that how an Italian system works? I wonder if the output is the same as American units?"

Giorgio shrugged and looked at the women

who were standing behind Hal. "Yes, I think so. I just need to grab some tools."

Getting what he needed, Giorgio turned back to the house with the new guest following in his wake. The bag he dropped hadn't moved, and Hal hadn't come back to fetch it. Apparently, that was to be left to his wife, who was now looking despondent and somewhat crushed by her husband's actions.

Maia wasn't quite sure what to say, so she made the simplest of offers.

"Can I help you with the luggage?" she asked quietly.

Lori looked close to tears and she bit her lip, casting her eyes downwards.

"Ten years. This is our tenth anniversary. We honeymooned here - in Sorrento. I thought that coming back here would..." Lori swallowed hard. "But no, he wants to fix the goddamned air conditioning."

Maia leaned forward and picked up the bag that Hal had dropped. "Maybe he just wants to be helpful?"

But Lori rolled her eyes. "*Right.* That's what it is. Him being *helpful*. Because at home if I have a sink clogged or need something done around the house, he simply jumps at the opportunity to help me." Lori's voice was thick with sarcasm and Maia felt immediately awkward. She had just met them after all, and was unsure what to do with the woman's candidness about her marriage.

"Well, all marriages have their rough spots," Maia said kindly.

"Really, it's okay. I'm used to this crap." She looked at the scenery around her, as if noticing it for the first time. "This place is gorgeous though…"

"Is there anything else I can do to help?" Maia asked - it didn't seem as if they had any more to carry inside, just the two bags.

The woman smiled. "Possibly, yes." She looked over Maia's shoulder at the house. "Do you by chance have any wine in there?"

Maia emitted a laugh.

Errant handyman husband aside, she knew she would get along with Lori Parish just fine.

CHAPTER 7

*H*al looked very satisfied with himself, when a little later he pronounced that the job was done and that they would once again have cool air in Villa Azalea.

Giorgio on the other hand, looked frazzled and weary. Maia was betting that Hal wasn't as big of a help as he thought he was.

"Well, that's fantastic news," she said as she placed a hand in front of a vent—feeling immediate relief when cold air hit her skin. She turned to where Lori was sitting at the kitchen table, drinking her requested glass of wine.

Maia had learned an awful lot about her new guest in the time that it had taken for Hal and Giorgio to do their work. She had discovered they were indeed the same age, both were childfree, and indeed of Irish descent, although Lori had lived in the United States her entire life.

However, there was one major difference between the two of them—where Maia had a happy marriage; it seemed that Lori had spent the last couple years of her relationship with Hal sailing troubled seas.

As she drank her wine, she was more than happy to divulge the fact that her marriage wasn't blissful, and that she was using this trip as a last ditch effort to reignite the spark—or else.

Maia wasn't entirely sure what "or else" meant, but she knew that its connotation didn't bode well for the future if Hal didn't turn into a devoted and attentive husband.

"Anyway, now that's fixed, I'm sure you are both ready to have some fun." Maia had discovered that the couple didn't fly in to Italy that day—therefore, neither one should be suffering any jetlag from their journey. If anything, she was well aware that Lori was eager to get out and see the sites. "We have some bikes here that you can borrow if you like —those are great for getting around the area. Or there is a vineyard actually right down the road within walking distance." Maia smiled at the couple hoping she was effectively pulling off the role of hospitality manager and tour director. "What do you think? It's a beautiful day, perfectl for exploring."

Lori was nodding eagerly in agreement, but when Maia looked at Hal, she was met with a wide yawn.

"Yeah not right now," he said. "I'm beat. I think I'm going to go take a nap or something."

And Lori's face once again fell. Maia immediately felt sad for the woman—disappointment was clear on her face.

How could her husband not see how thoughtless he was being?

Seeing Lori swallow hard, Maia clasped and unclasped her hands, wondering what to do. But then Lori spoke. "Hal, you slept late today. Why don't we go out and do something. There's no use wasting our time—not that this house isn't lovely—but I thought we were going to find that little trattoria that we visited on our honeymoon? Why don't we do that?

Maia said we could borrow the bikes—it won't be far from here."

But Hal was already shaking his head. "I really need a nap. Why don't you go?" he said, turning toward the hallway. "Which way is our room? You brought the bags in, right?"

Maia felt herself holding her breath. If Jim ever pulled something like that, she would have exploded.

But Lori didn't offer fireworks; instead she took a slug of her wine and turned to look out the window. "Yeah. It's that way. Down the hallway, second door on the left. Enjoy your nap." Lori looked back at Maia pointedly—she was refusing to meet her husband's eyes. "I hope you don't mind if I go take a walk. I need some air."

CHAPTER 8

Camilla joined Maia in the kitchen shortly afterwards. She had contemplated going out and keeping Lori company, but it seemed clear that the woman needed some alone time.

"How is everyone getting on?" Camilla asked.

Maia shrugged and looked out into the garden, where Lori had found a home with her glass of wine.

"I don't know really—I feel like this current group might be good for reality TV, truth be told."

Camilla joined her at the window and peered out.

"Is she out there by herself?" Maia nodded. "Well, that's not much fun. Come on. Let's get to know her." Maia was about to call out and tell her friend that she suspected Lori might need time to organise her thoughts, but before she knew it Camilla was out the door, calling over an introduction.

"Oh bloody hell," Maia cursed quietly. "Well, if you can't beat them …" She grabbed the open bottle of wine.

Moments later, the trio found themselves in the middle of comfortable conversation. Whatever melancholy Lori had been feeling obviously started to dissipate once Maia offered her another glass.

"So tell me Maia, how did you end up here?" Lori inquired.

Clearing her throat, she offered the short version, and Lori murmured her condolences when she got to the part about Jim's passing.

"He sounds like he was a great man," she said with a small smile. "Anyone who follows a dream like this …I really admire you two. I can't imagine ever living anywhere else except Florida."

Maia shrugged. "I always thought that

about us too. It was hard for me to wrap my head around leaving the place I had lived for my entire life. But now, I don't know if I could ever go back to Ireland. This is home now."

Lori nodded and sat back in her chair, getting comfortable. "Not a bad place to hang your hat, if I do say so myself."

"You are from Florida?" said Camilla excitedly. "I have always wanted to go there."

"To visit Disney World I suppose?"

But Camilla tilted her head. "No, no to Miami Beach. I am not a child after all."

Maia laughed. It was true that she often forgot that Camilla wasn't a teenager, but a woman in her mid twenties. "But I mean, maybe I will go to Disney too. I love the princesses."

"There's a lot of fun things to do in the Sunshine State," offered Lori. "Not that I do many of them anymore…"

"So how did you and Hal get together?" Maia asked, hoping to change the subject to a happier topic.

With that question, Lori's eyes took on a faraway look—and Maia knew that she had asked the right thing. It was apparent that she still very much loved her husband, but was living vicariously through her memories.

"It was eleven years ago," Lori said. "We didn't date for long or have an extended engagement. I mean, we were both already in our mid-thirties. And when you get to be that age, you know when it's right. You don't have to spend years trying to figure it out. With Hal, from day one, I knew it was right. He used to be so awfully romantic."

Apparently, Hal and Lori had met in Miami Beach—and she did a good job of painting the location for Camilla. But while Camilla wanted to know about the city's party scene, Lori was frank that she couldn't really offer knowledge about that because while she had been planning to go out with her girlfriends that night, those plans had been derailed—as she had instead gone for a beautiful sunset ride in his boat.

"By the end of the night, I just knew. He was so spontaneous back then. Nothing would have stopped him from saying, 'Hey, let's take the boat down the coast to Key West,' or 'why not a trip to the Bahamas this weekend?' Even our wedding was a bit spur of the moment. We flew to Vegas and eloped." Lori smiled with the memory. "We didn't want a big wedding—we wanted to keep it small and spend our money on the honeymoon. Here. It was perfect."

Maia nodded in agreement. "Jim and I were the same way. Small wedding, just our family and close friends. And then a wonderful extended honeymoon."

But Camilla tisked. "Small weddings. When I get married, I will have a huge wedding. If I tried to do something small, my family would disown me," she grinned. "I want a dress with a thirty foot train. It will fill the aisle of the cathedral."

"And I have no doubt that the cathedral will be St. Peter's Basilica," Maia chided and the trio laughed loudly. "Do you want some more wine?" she asked Lori.

But before the other woman could answer, Amelia stepped outside.

"Oh dear, I'm so sorry Amelia, I hope we didn't disturb you, I'm afraid we were being quite loud."

"Not at all. It was time for me to get up anyway—I just wanted to get some fresh air."

Quickly, Maia introduced her guests to

each other and taking a seat, Amelia appeared much more relaxed than she had been earlier that day.

"So what brings you here, hon?" Lori asked.

Remembering the conversation from earlier, Maia quickly tried to figure out how to deflect the topic—it had been apparent that Amelia wasn't overly excited to attend her friend's wedding.

But Camilla, who had obviously forgotten the young woman's discomfort, spoke first, "She is here to attend a friend's wedding," she said simply.

Amelia looked pale

"Well, what a perfect place to get married," Lori noted.

Amelia looked around and shrugged her agreement. "I suppose. But no offense, it wouldn't have been my choice."

Camilla shot a knowing look at Maia. "Well then it's lucky, yes? That you are just friends with the groom."

A cloud passed over Amelia's face, and she turned away from Camilla's inquiring eyes, casting a longing look over the Bay of Naples.

She looked as if she wanted to be anywhere except here.

"Well, actually, that's the thing.... It was … supposed to be me. My friend, the groom, he's… he's actually, my ex. And that's why I am here, to watch him marry someone else."

CHAPTER 9

The three woman stared in silence at Amelia, all (except Camilla it seemed) surprised by what she had just revealed.

Amelia on the other hand, suddenly looked light as a feather—as if she had been looking for a way to get that little revelation off her chest.

Lori was the first to speak. "He's your ex? And you are *going to* his wedding?"

Amelia took a long slug from the wine glass. She seemed to take a minute to ponder the taste of the red liquid, and once again threw a look out over the Bay, as if debating whether or not to answer the question.

Finally, she nodded. "Yes. Aaron. He and I were engaged actually. And now he is marrying someone else. She's his co-worker. They were always good 'friends' when we were together."

"Are you saying he cheated on you with this woman?" inquired Camilla, disgust thick in her voice.

Amelia shrugged and brushed a loose strand of blonde hair from her face. "I really have no idea. It's just awfully convenient, I suppose. All I know is that he ended it with me —he said he wasn't ready to get married. I'd just bought my dress the day before. Everything was set. And he said he wasn't ready. You would have thought this might have dawned on him before he proposed to me, don't you?"

Camilla was nodding her head vehemently, agreeing with everything that Amelia was saying. "So what happened next?" she asked, seemingly on tenterhooks.

Taking a deep breath, Amelia continued. "He had asked me to be his 'friend'. That he still loved me. That I was still the *best* person in his life." Then she let out a small shudder. "But within six months he was engaged to *her*."

Maia sat silently shaking her head. She sometimes couldn't believe the drama in some relationships—and she knew that she had been lucky. Her relationship with Jim had always been drama free. Quietly she asked the question that all of them were thinking.

"So Amelia, then really - why are you here?"

The British girl shrugged. "To be honest, now I don't know. When the invite showed up in the post what I really wanted to do was put it through a shredder. I honestly saw red. But I didn't want to be that person. I decided at the last moment to come. But I couldn't stay at the hotel with the wedding party. His parents would be there, and I always loved his parents. I knew I would see the pity on their faces. So I suppose, to answer your question, I came because I needed to see it happen. I needed the visual confirmation. I suppose I am a glutton for punishment really, voluntarily attending a wedding to watch the love of my life marry another woman."

Suddenly, tears welled up in her eyes and spilled down her cheeks.

Maia immediately rushed forward to put

her arms around the young woman. As cleansing as her speech and her explanation about why she was in Italy might have been, it had obviously taken its toll on her.

"Oh sweetheart, I'm so sorry. I can say you are very strong being here, attending this wedding. I don't know if I would have been able to do the same. What you are doing is very brave," said Maia kindly.

Amelia sniffled. "My best friend said I was just sadistic."

"No," insisted Maia. "You're not. I think you have a good philosophy actually—looking for closure. But if you really want to move on, you have to realise that just seeing him get married isn't enough. I think there are plenty of people out there, men and women both, who have pined over someone unattainable—only to have their hearts broken time and again."

Lori was nodding, agreeing with Maia's words. "Watch him get married. But you have to find a reason to check out before you head to the wedding, if you get my drift."

Amelia wiped her eyes and furrowed her brow. "And how do I do that?"

Lori smiled. "I always say that the best way

to get over a guy is to get under another. And hey, this is the perfect place for an Italian fling."

Maia rolled her eyes and laughed. "Amelia, I don't want to sound like an old maid—and while Lori means well—I'm not sure if immediately diving into another relationship, fling or not, is the best advice. I think what she meant to say is you have to figure out what makes you happy, outside of the way you might have felt, or feel, for this Aaron. I think you should figure out how to love yourself first, that's the way to get closure. Because a woman who has confidence in who she is and what she has to offer, will never allow herself to be taken advantage of—and her happiness will never be held in the balance because of the actions of someone else."

Camilla was once again smiling and nodding. "She's right, you know. In my life, I never let any man be in charge of my happiness. And they follow me around. I pick who makes me happy. And he is lucky for it."

Maia laughed loudly. If one thing was for sure, Camilla had no deficiency in the confidence department.

She looked at the others. "I suppose now

and again, all of us could do with a reminder to never put the key to our happiness in someone else's pocket."

CHAPTER 10

*L*ater, Maia was keeping a watchful eye on the kitchen door as she and Camilla began the process of making dinner for the house.

Amelia had been gone a while now, had left for a walk to "clear her head" but Maia still felt a great deal of concern for her.

While she herself had never had children, she was pretty sure that Amelia was of the age where she could in fact, be her daughter—and feeling some maternal concern over the state that Amelia's heart was in.

No one deserved to be put through such an ordeal, Maia thought to herself as she breaded chicken breast filets, to feel like you have to watch the love of your life get married, just to find closure.

She was sure that she could never put herself through the same sort of scenario—she certainly could have never watched Jim marry another woman.

Do you think I gave her good advice, honey? she asked, turning her thoughts to the ether. It sounded like Amelia had been put through the ringer by this fellow, and while it was true that she wasn't sure if he had been cheating on her with his co-worker, the signs pointed to this.

Maia also felt confident that if there was one spot where Amelia might be able to find peace, it was here.

Maybe it was a blessing then, that the wedding happened to be taking place in Sorrento. Maybe Amelia was meant to come, and stay here in the home that Maia and Jim had created, just to find herself.

She felt comforted by the thought. Maybe she had been right to do this.

It looked like all this was about more than just providing shelter and a bed to weary travellers. Thinking of the diverse little group that was lodging in her home at that moment, Maia couldn't help but wonder if maybe they all weren't there for a bigger purpose…

"Oh, he's back! He's back!" Camilla exclaimed, quickly turning her attention from the kitchen window to her cleavage. Standing up straighter and adjusting the neckline of the top she was wearing, she then brushed her dark hair back and fluffed it. Tossing it seductively, she looked at Maia. "How do I look?"

"What do you want me to say? Hot?"

"Yes. Am I hot?" pressed Camilla.

Maia nodded. "Yes, you're definitely hot."

In more ways than one, she thought with a smile.

"Good. I hope he likes *Pollo alla Cacciatora*."

Maia hoped for Jacob's sake that he was hungry this evening—otherwise Camilla was going to be completely unforgiving if another dish was wasted on him.

The kitchen door opened shortly thereafter, and Jacob entered. His eyes quickly darted around the room, assessing the situation and finally fell on Camilla, who was all but preening under his gaze. "Welcome back Jacob

," she smiled sweetly. "You have great timing. We are just finishing dinner. I hope you are hungry now."

Jacob instinctively put a hand over his stomach and Camilla's eyes followed, no doubt imagining taut six-pack abs.

For a moment however, he looked poised to decline the invite, but then Maia intervened.

"I hope you know it's bad luck to turn down the culinary efforts of an Italian woman two times in a row," she said over her shoulder. "If your family is Italian that should be part of your genetic makeup."

Jacob opened his mouth to probably argue that point, but then he shut it again and provided them both with an unexpected, but incredibly handsome, smile. It wasn't the first time they saw him smile, but it was definitely the first time that it looked genuine.

He put up his hands, signalling defeat.

"I think you might be right Maia. I surrender. And yes I'll eat. Sorry, sitting down for dinner isn't something that I think about a lot. I haven't eaten since I was on the plane, and that wasn't much."

Camilla looked confused. "How on earth do

you not think about eating? And you call yourself Italian? Now go, sit."

Jacob did as he was told, taking a seat at the kitchen table. After considering Maia's offer of a beverage and settling on a Peroni, because he said he "needed it," he sat back in his chair, and rolled up the sleeves of the white dress shirt he was wearing.

"Thanks," he said, taking a sip of the beer from the bottle. He swallowed and took a deep breath.

Maia went about setting the table for six, anticipating that all of her guests would eventually sit down and eat at some point.

"Been a bit of a hard day then?" she commented off-handedly, hoping she wasn't overstepping her boundaries.

But he appeared to be a bit more relaxed than he had been earlier.

"Understatement of the year. Kinda throws your life out of whack, when you wake up one morning and all is normal, but by the end of the day you are on a flight to Italy. Not the best time honestly, and it's hard for me to get away even when I plan a trip for months."

Maia nodded politely.

"So is it your job then? The reason you don't think about eating?" Camilla asked, unconcerned about protocol.

Though Maia agreed he seemed like your typical New Yorker, fast, urgent-minded, short of time.

"I suppose you could say that. I'm a hedge fund manager."

"Wall Street?"

He ran a lazy hand through his hair. "Yes. Go ahead, you can cast the stereotypes out there right now. I don't mind."

Maia smiled and shook her head. "Not my style."

Camilla placed a bottle of sparkling water on the table. "So you had to leave New York fast then?"

Jacob shrugged. "If I'm being honest, I wasn't going to come at all but for pressure from a persistent woman to do the right thing. And like you said Maia, it's never wise to argue with Italian women."

Camilla's eyes darted to Jacob's left hand.

"Pressure, from your wife?" she queried. She knew some men didn't wear a wedding ring. "Or your girlfriend?" she added coyly.

But Jacob shook his head and took another sip of his Peroni. "I'm single," he smiled, his eyes involuntarily and briefly appreciating the cleavage that Camilla had been intent on showing off. "It was my sister actually. She lives in Boston, but she has been here for about a month, helping out. She insisted that I get my ass over."

Maia grimaced. "So your father is badly ill then?" she commented gently.

"He's been dying for years," Jacob said, bitterness creeping into his voice. "But Adriana, my sister, said this time it's for real. He has cancer." Maia exchanged a glance with Camilla—where their conversation had been easygoing, awkwardness had now crept in. "Sorry, it's just, my dad and I don't get along."

Maia pondered what to say next. "You don't have to talk about it if you don't want to."

Jacob thanked Camilla as she placed the chicken breast and pasta dish on his plate and offered him salad and garlic bread. He picked up his fork and sat silent for a moment, as if figuring out whether or not he did want to speak.

Finally, he took a deep breath. "My mom,

sister and I, we moved to New York when I was four, Adriana was seven. You see, my dad, he had left my mother—and she found that she didn't have a bunch of options here in Italy as a single mother. So she took us and left. He didn't fight her on it. And he started a new family—just like that, like we had never existed. But my mom, she was suddenly responsible for rebuilding her entire life, with two little kids, in a foreign country, all by herself. She worked as a cleaning lady, scrimped and saved, did everything she could for us, just to get by—he never helped. Hell, he could barely even be bothered to send us a birthday card." He took a bite of his meal and his eyebrows rose in appreciation. "This is great, seriously - fantastic," he said to Camilla, who looked as proud as punch at his compliment. "Anyway my mom always did well by us, and I have always been intent on paying her back for her sacrifices—I bought her a townhouse in Brooklyn, she wanted something with a yard. I make sure she always has what she needs and more. But *him*, well, I don't have a lot of patience for him. Real men don't leave their wives, abandon their families. That's just how I feel."

Maia put her fork on her plate as she considered Jacob's admission. It was all so sad.

"So your sister is closer to him, yes?" Camilla ventured.

Jacob nodded. "Adriana's always been a more forgiving person. But I suppose she also remembers some of the happy times with him. She was older than me—I just don't remember him being anything other than a jerk—and my mom's struggle, after he left us, that's always been forefront in my mind. Adriana thinks that she convinced me to come over here out of some sort of duty—but I can't say that I did... for that reason at least."

Maia finished chewing the food in her mouth and swallowed. "So why did you come?" she asked tentatively.

Jacob seemed to consider his answer. A beam of sunlight suddenly entered from the kitchen window, striking the table where they sat—its intensity fading against the pale pink backdrop of the summer sky.

"I suppose I came because I wanted to show him I am successful, and that I don't pity him—

that we don't have a relationship and we never will, because soon, he'll be dead, and I'll go on with my life like he never existed."

Maia felt a bit blind-sided by just how frank this admission was. "Are you sure you want to feel that way?" she asked.

But Jacob didn't have time to answer because the backdoor opened and Amelia strode in. Her cheeks were rosy and she looked the tiniest bit windblown. She definitely looked... *happier.*

"Oh!" she stumbled. "I seem to keep interrupting when people are eating."

"Nonsense," said Maia, jumping up. "It's what you do in Italy—eat—several times per day. Please, sit down. What can I get you to drink?"

And just like that the increasingly difficult conversation with Jacob was forgotten—Maia didn't think it was right to continue, not with the new introduction of Amelia to the group, nor did she think it appropriate to ask Amelia how she was feeling.

So the table kept to neutral topics—jobs, hobbies, favourite travel spots and the like.

Through it all, Hal and Lori never showed

up for dinner. Maia was pretty sure they were both still in the house—she didn't think they had left.

Deciding to check on them later, she put some food away for them, just in case.

CHAPTER 11

When dinner was over, Camilla began cleaning up with Amelia's help, and Maia walked in the direction of the Parrish's room to let them know that there was food if they wanted it.

But as she neared their door, she was immediately hit with the sound of raised, albeit muffled, voices coming from within.

"No, *you* don't understand Hal. You are one of the most insensitive people I have ever met. We are in Italy for God's sakes. And what do you do? You want to fix the goddamn air conditioning at the place we are staying. Why don't you just say it? That you don't want to be here? That you have already checked out of this marriage?" cried Lori.

Maia felt a surge of embarrassment rush through her and she slowly stepped away.

As the argument became more heated, she didn't want to be caught eavesdropping should either one of them open the door, and she also knew that this was none of her business. She hoped that her footsteps were not making any noise on the wooden floors beneath.

"What do you want from me Lori? Just tell me and I'll do it. And why would you say that? That I've checked out. I swear to God, I can't do anything right. I really can't, not with you, not anymore. I agreed to come to Italy. I agreed to this guesthouse. I agreed to this downtime because you said we needed it—I don't know what else to do for you!"

Back in the kitchen, Maia couldn't help but feel upset over what she had heard between the fighting couple.

She excused herself and went outside, where the cool evening breeze whipped tendrils of hair round her temples and the scent of lemons fragranced the air.

She walked down the path away from the

house, toward the road and the cliff side, determined to find some solitude to clear her head.

And she knew just the spot.

Finding her way easily to a small overlook that gave a clear view of the Naples city lights at night, she felt herself calming as she walked.

However, she was surprised to find that when she reached her destination she was not alone—Jacob had apparently found her secret place too.

And he was so fully immersed in taking in the view that he didn't hear Maia's footsteps as she approached.

"Hello," she said softly, announcing her presence. She certainly didn't want to shock anyone when they were standing that close to the edge of a hillside. "I didn't realise this place was that easy to find," she said with a smile.

Jacob turned around, finally realising he was no longer alone.

"Oh, hey, I'm sorry, I was just walking a bit and I stumbled upon this area. A bit off the beaten path, yes? I hope you don't mind. If you needed some time alone, I can go," he offered.

But Maia waved a dismissive hand. "Please, not a problem at all. It will be nice to have some company here. I haven't in some time." She took a seat on the grass. "Care to join me? Best seat in the house." She patted the soft ground next to her, and Jacob dutifully sat.

He sighed deeply as he got comfortable and cast his eyes out over the Neapolitan vista. The seashore was dotted with lights and low lying buildings filled the Napoli harbour. The sky had not fully given up the setting sun, and off into the West, the last remnants of daylight headed south.

"It sure looks different - from the skyline of New York that is."

"It is quite different yes," agreed Maia.

"Have you been? To New York that is?" Jacob asked to which she offered an affirmative nod.

"Twice, but not recently. Once as a teenager, and once with my husband, Jim, right after we were married. It's a great city. I don't suppose I could live there though. I like the quiet this place offers. I feel like I might be a fish out of water in a city like that," she smiled, turning her eyes to Jacob, who was now looking back at the metropolis beneath.

He had a strong Italian profile—like many

of the men she saw here each day. There was no denying he was handsome; she could see why Camilla was attracted, but he was more refined than most of the men she met.

Probably because he was a full on New Yorker and had been his whole life. But, Maia knew that Italian passion still drove through his veins. His feelings toward his father were evidence of that.

"Do you remember Sorrento at all?" she asked. "I know you said you were very young when you left."

Jacob shrugged. "There are snippets, I guess. Little memories. I don't know if they're real or if it's something I saw in one of my mom's photo albums. Honestly, probably one of my clearer memories is of going to Pompeii, probably right before we left for the U.S. I remember thinking it was absolutely hilarious that there were pictures of naked people on the walls of one of the buildings. I now know it was a brothel that serviced the city," he laughed. "But I was just a little boy who thought it was funny—these naked people painted on the walls, all twisted around each other. I didn't know what the purpose of the establishment - I guess you might say - was." He laughed. "It's weird the things you remember you know?"

Maia nodded and smiled. "I get that. Little random things—especially when it comes to my husband. Like the time we got into an argument about something while sitting at the dinner table—I can't even recall what—but during the whole thing, he had this piece of corn stuck on his cheek. And I was so mad at him that I just let it sit there. It honestly made me feel better. It's hard to argue with someone who has food on their face. But I always wondered, after he died, why did I remember *that*? Out of all things …what was its significance to my life?"

Taking a deep breath of sea air and closing her eyes, Maia listened for the sounds that floated up from the valley beneath.

When she opened her eyes again she shrugged.

"I'm glad I do remember though. Even with Jim gone. It's little things like that, that pepper my thoughts. They help keep him alive to me."

The pair sat in silence for a moment and

when Jacob finally spoke, his statement caught her unawares.

"You asked me a question earlier, at dinner, about the way I felt toward my father. You asked me if I was sure I wanted to feel that way."

Maia shifted uncomfortably. "I'm sorry, I shouldn't have said that. It's not my place ..."

"No, it's okay. It's what brought me out here. I needed to think," Jacob said evenly. "But can I ask you a question?" She nodded her approval. "Have you ever had to try to forgive someone for a lifetime of unhappiness?"

Maia tilted her head. "Are *you* unhappy though? You don't seem that way to me."

Jacob tucked his feet up closer to his body and wrapped his arms around his legs. "No, I'm not unhappy. I have everything I could want in life—great career, money to buy whatever I want, companionship if I want it, friends. And quite honestly, if it were just about me, I probably wouldn't give him another thought. But it's my mom. It's about *her*. She spent the majority of the prime years of her life unhappy, overworked, caring for two children alone. I remember her crying at night when she thought Adriana and I were asleep. I remember her stressing over money. I guess that's what I find unforgivable."

It was an honest answer, Maia thought. But she also believed there was something out of kilter with his line of thinking.

"What about your mother? What does she think of him?"

Jacob sighed. "That's what I don't get. When Adriana was pressuring me to come over here, Mom told me I should come too. I mean, why? I told her if it was so important that I come here, then why didn't she come with me? To watch the old man die, to get that closure. She said that closure occurred for her when she left Italy. That she didn't need to mourn him again."

Maia smiled, understanding what Jacob was missing. "Your mother sounds like a very wise woman."

"How so?" he asked.

"It sounds to me like your mother finished mourning for her relationship with your father years ago. And what you interpreted as her dealing with a broken heart, might really just have been a woman who was doing her best to handle the stresses of making a new life for herself after the plans she thought were set in stone, crumbled before her eyes. What you perceived as unhappiness, regret and loneliness could very well have been something different."

Jacob furrowed his brow. "How do you know that?"

"Because I've been through it," Maia answered simply.

Thinking of the painful time immediately after Jim's passing, she took a deep breath and willed herself not to cry.

"I had a great love in my life. And no, Jim didn't leave me, but after he died, I knew that there was nothing I could do to bring him back. I could wish on a star all night every night, but that wouldn't change a thing about my situation. But what I could do is make a new life for myself, decide how I could make myself happy in this new reality. There have been nights where I have lain awake crying because of stress. How was I going to keep this place? What was I going to do when the savings account ran out? What happens next? I'm only in my forties - prime years of my life. And I'm all alone," Maia admitted sadly. "And there have been times where I have felt mad at Jim. It was irrational, I know. After all, he went to the doctor, he never had any health problems. That heart attack wasn't his fault. But I have carried on, because I had to. No, I don't have to support children but I didn't want to lose this place." She motioned in the direction of the farmhouse. "That was Jim's dream and Jim's baby—and it became mine. The heart is resilient, Jacob, I think your mother is proof of that. She made her choices. You shouldn't fight her battles for her—she has done that already."

"So you think she wasn't just crying over him? All of those years."

Maia shrugged. "I'm sure she did her fair share of crying over him too. Tell me, does your mother have anyone in her life now? Anyone special?"

Jacob nodded. "Yes, a nice guy. His name is Peter. He's a widower. They've been seeing each other for seven years or so. But she has no interest in getting married—Peter's asked her many times."

Grinning, Maia said, "Then I don't think you should worry about your mom's happiness any longer—she sounds like she knows what she wants and who she is, although you are a good son to be concerned. I think maybe you should focus on your own feelings about your father, and not project your worries over your mother into it. What happens if you allow this grudge to fester? Let me tell you. He dies. And whatever sins he's committed in his life, whatever bad judgment or bad choices he made, that all dies with him. If you are religious, then you have your own beliefs over what happens after that. If you're not, his life becomes dust. But Jacob, you get to *live*. And that hate, those bad feelings you carry? That festers and grows and soon overpowers you. It becomes part of *you*—and then, well, maybe you aren't any better than your father. But he's gone—and you're walking the earth with blackness inside that threatens the very happiness you could achieve in your life. Just forgive your father, Jacob. You don't have to profess your love to him. You don't have to cry by his bedside. But forgive. And let those bad feelings die when he does."

Jacob was silent, and he put his head in his hands and covered his eyes. Maia didn't think he was crying, but he was definitely working her words over in his mind.

"Just think about it," she said, putting a comforting hand on his back. She then stood up and prepared to take her leave, pretty sure Jacob needed to be alone for a bit. "Life's too short. You can't change the past, but you can decide how you want to live in the future. Your father no longer has power over you. Unless you give it to him."

CHAPTER 12

Maia got up early the next morning—practically rising with the sun—determined to get a jumpstart on the day.

She had a to-do list that felt a mile long as her tasks had seemingly multiplied. Not only did she have to attend to the normal everyday chores around the house, but she had to now also ensure that her guests were happy and well taken care of.

She exited the house and headed directly to the roadside stand to check stock, in order to let Camilla know what was needed, but also begin canning some olives and picking some lemons herself.

Once finished, she exited the small booth and stood in front of it, inspecting its appearance.

"I really think I need to ask Giorgio to put another coat of paint on it," she commented to herself, before turning her attention to the surrounding azalea bushes. "And those are getting way too overgrown. A woman's work is never done…" she sighed.

Deciding at once that there was no time like the present, she headed to the garden shed before returning with a pair of pruning shears and a basket.

One thing was for certain, very little went to waste around this house. Whatever she cut off the bushes would end up decorating the interior of the villa in fragrant bouquets.

"Nice flowers," said a voice from behind her. "What are they?"

Startled, Maia turned around quickly to find Hal watching her work. "Sorry, I didn't hear you approach." She noticed that she was holding up her shears defensively as if ready to defend herself.

"I didn't mean to scare you," he smiled kindly. "My apologies. I was just out wandering around and I didn't realise anyone else was up yet."

"Ah, an early riser then," Maia smiled. "And these are azaleas to answer your question." She turned back to her work. "Do you mind running back to the shed over there and getting me another basket? There's one just inside the door."

Hal agreed and did as he was bid. When he returned a moment later with the empty container, he helpfully moved the full basket of azaleas out of Maia's way.

"Are these going somewhere?"

"Yes, into the house. I'll make some bouquets. No sense wasting them. They're too pretty." A beat of silence passed between the pair before Maia spoke again. "So Lori's still sleeping?"

"Yes she's um, a bit tired," he stuttered and Maia had the immediate flashback of overhearing the couple arguing the evening before.

"So do you both have plans today?" she inquired, hoping the answer would be yes, for Lori's sake alone. The woman seemed at the end of her tether.

But Hal shrugged in a non-committal manner.

"I don't know. Maybe she has plans, there are things that she wants to do and whatnot, but I really don't know why *I'm* here," he sighed, putting his hands in his pockets. "I wouldn't say that my wife and I are getting along too well right now."

Maia tilted her head and put her pruning shears down for a moment, her attention turned fully to Hal.

"Lori and I talked a bit yesterday afternoon, while you were napping," she admitted. "I told her that all marriages go through rough patches. I really think it's just about figuring out how to work through some of those times."

Hal crossed his arms and leaned against the side of the lemon stand.

"Yeah, I know," he said sadly. "And maybe I was hoping that just being in a different place, away from home, would be an instant fix. You know, like a vacation high of sorts? But if anything, she seems unhappier now."

Maia nodded as Hal continued.

"You know the thing is, we both spend so

much of our time consumed with our careers, - and I don't care what she says - Lori is just as committed to hers as I am. Having kids was never a priority for us, and we met at a time when we were both older, knew what we wanted out of life, had the means to do things. But then I guess, something changed. Most days now I feel like we live separate lives. Like we live together and go out to dinner, and do all the stuff that married couples do, but at the same time we exist in two completely separate universes. We might be talking over breakfast, but our minds are in different places, already going about our day. That's how it feels to me anyhow."

Maia considered Hal's statement, and then took in his appearance. He was well turned out, in a polo shirt and khaki shorts, but he looked tired. She wondered if Lori noticed that—the fatigue in his eyes and the lines on his forehead. It was clear that he understood his wife was unhappy; he just wasn't sure about what to do about it.

"You look like you could use some coffee. Why don't you come into the house? I had a pot brewing before I came out here."

Hal agreed, and helped Maia carry one of the overflowing flower baskets. Once they reached the kitchen, she took the load before grabbing a mug and pouring him a cup of coffee. Settling him in at the kitchen table, she began pulling vases from cabinets—she needed to get these azaleas in water.

Hal sipped his coffee and nodded his head appreciatively. "That's great. Thank you. You know, I love my wife. I really do. Please don't get me wrong there, no matter what she told you."

"Oh, I think she knows you love her," Maia said, hoping her words were true. "I suspect you guys might just be in a slump, that's all. You simply need to make an effort, change things around, do something different. Maybe the two of you need to remember how to be a couple again. If you are on different wavelengths like you say, maybe it's time to start crossing your wires again?" She smiled, hoping Hal didn't think she was implying some sort of sexual innuendo.

He tapped his fingers on the kitchen table.

"So, what do you suggest? I mean, I'm a

man; you have to talk to me like I'm five—or so my wife thinks."

Maia barked a laugh as she finished arranging the flowers in one vase.

"Well Lori said yesterday she wanted to visit some trattoria you'd been to before? And she was also interested in a bike ride. What's stopping you from doing that?"

Hal shrugged and looked uncomfortable.

"I don't know, I guess there is something in me that feels like situations like that ... like going on a bike ride just because you're on vacation is contrived. We would never do that back home. That's just not us."

Biting her lip, Maia mumbled, "Hmm." She remembered what Lori had said the day before about how Hal used to be spontaneous—she wondered what had happened to that sense of adventure.

Life, apparently.

She took the vase of flowers she was working on and placed it on the sideboard, taking a moment to admire it before she spoke again.

"But isn't that the point of escaping from the day to day? To do something out of the ordinary? It's called a 'vacation' because it is - a break from the norm. For example, you don't worry about things like air conditioning going on the blink, because you are too busy looking for your next adventure to care."

Hal grimaced. "Hey, I was only trying to help."

"And *I* appreciated it, thank you. But now's not the time to worry about practical stuff—it *is* time to worry about your wife, and what's happening out there." She pointed beyond the window. "Apparently, the two of you fell in love with this location and even more in love with each other, before. Why can't you do it again?"

Offering another shrug, Hal stayed silent and pondered this.

Maia took her mug of coffee and sat down at the table beside him.

"When Jim, my husband and I, lived in Ireland, before we came here, all we did was work, work, work. I was a graphic designer at a busy company in Dublin. Jim worked in finance. He had always talked about wanting to move here when he retired." She laughed at the memory. "I remember at first thinking he was just spouting off big dreams. It was only after I saw the brochures laid out all over this exact same table," she motioned to the surface beneath their coffee cups, "did I realise he was serious. Buying an old farmhouse, in Italy of all places—well, I thought he was quite crazy—the pure spontaneity of it! Can you imagine? But, supporting wife that I was, well, I finally agreed.

But then, when we got here, we worked harder than we ever worked in our corporate jobs, I think. In fact, I know we did. But something else happened in the midst of all that. Jim started doing things that I would have never pictured him doing when we lived in Dublin. Like one day, I walked into the kitchen, and the place was just a mess. We were in the process of stripping back the floors, and I knew it was going to be a very long and trying day.

But then Jim said, 'No, we are doing something different today,' and he held up this picnic basket. A picnic? I thought, seriously - in the middle of all this chaos? But that's just what we did, after he convinced me that the work could wait until another day, that there would *always* be more to do in a place like this, but that ultimately, we had come here for a reason."

"So what did you do?" Hal asked.

"We went on that picnic," Maia laughed. "We trotted off down the hillside and spent the entire day basking in the sunshine, eating bread and cheese and drinking wine. It was a perfect day." She paused, recalling the time, reliving the wonderful memory.

"And Jim was right. I can't believe it took us leaving Dublin and the hustle and bustle of our everyday lives to realise that sometimes, you need to just stop and connect with the person you love. Jim said one time - it was after we finished renovating that room, 'Well this looks great, but I've had enough for one day,' and I was so intent on just admiring our work, looking at the new paint, and walking around on the floorboards we'd just uncovered, and all this *stuff*, that Jim finally had to pull me from the room. He said, 'I love what we did, but it won't keep me warm at night—you will.' I guess my point is, this place allowed him and I, even for a short time, to find balance in our lives. I realise you and Lori aren't moving in," she smiled, "but maybe it can also work its magic on you two while you're here? If you let it."

Hal smiled. "So how do I get started on some of this Villa Azalea 'magic'?"

Laughing, Maia got up, and reached for the vase of flowers. "I thought you'd never ask…"

CHAPTER 13

When Lori opened her eyes, she felt momentarily discombobulated. As her mind snapped into motion, she remembered where she was—the Italian farmhouse in Sorrento. But what confused her now was the bouquet of fresh azaleas that had suddenly appeared on her bedside table. That hadn't been there the night before, when she had gone to bed angry next to Hal—the two of them sleeping with their backs turned to each other.

It had been a million miles from romantic. Some vacation!

She sat up and edged closer to the side of the bed, dipping her face into the fresh blooms, their fragrance all at once calming her. Lori looked behind her to Hal's side of the bed only to find it empty.

Getting up from bed and putting her robe on, she opened the door and padded down the hallway with bare feet. Entering the kitchen, she found it empty, but smelling of fresh coffee and hot bread. The sound of voices outside trickled into the house and she followed her ears.

Opening the kitchen door, she was immediately met with a cool summer's morning. The heat of the day had not yet found its way up the side of the mountain to the farmhouse. She was also welcomed by her husband and Maia sitting and chatting in the wooden lounge chairs that peppered the courtyard.

Feeling immediately annoyed, primarily that her husband could just get up and carry on with the landlady, happily relaxed when he couldn't do it with her, she was about to offer her displeasure when Hal cut her off, speaking first.

"There you are, honey," he smiled. "Good morning. I hope you liked your flowers."

Momentarily stunned, Lori opened and

closed her mouth—and then opened it again. "Those were from you?"

Hal nodded and Maia nudged him with her elbow.

"Yes, I was up early this morning and found Maia cutting them. I…helped. And I put some in your…our…room."

Lori tilted her head out of confusion. "You helped Maia cut flowers?" She couldn't believe her ears.

Hal shrugged, as if looking for a way to diminish his role, but Maia spoke before he could say a word.

"He did help me. And he also did something else. Hal why don't you tell her? Lori, would you like some coffee? I just brewed another pot, I'm afraid that Hal and I drank the first." Lori nodded her assent and Maia duly got up to go back into the house.

She plopped down in the chair next to Hal.

"What else did you do this morning?" she inquired, all the vitriol now gone from her voice and absent from her mind. She was curious to know what her husband had been up to while she had been sleeping.

He shifted in his seat. "Well, I um, cleaned

off the bikes that Maia mentioned yesterday. And I thought that maybe we could go on a picnic. Maia said there's a spot that she and her husband used to go to, and we are on vacation after all. I mean, unless you want to go to that trattoria first? We can save the picnic for another day…or…."

But Lori was smiling, a grin so genuine she resembled a child on Christmas morning.

"You want to go on a *picnic*? With *me*?"

Hal's face reddened and as Maia retreated inside, she smiled.

"Yes, Lori. You. I want to go on a picnic with *you*."

CHAPTER 14

Later that morning, Maia was manning the olive and lemon stand, when Jacob joined her, asking if she minded the company.

The pair chatted amicably for a while, avoiding mention of their conversation the night before, and bypassing the subject of his father, until Amelia also made her way outside.

"Maia, I was wondering if you knew where Le Sirenuse hotel is? How far it is from here, I mean." The girl was holding a piece of paper in her hand, which Maia assumed was the wedding invitation.

She nodded. "Further down the coast that way, in Positano."

"So I'll need a taxi?"

"Definitely. I can call one for you—get them to arrange to pick you back up at a certain time too, if you like?" Though Amelia didn't look too happy with that, likely Maia thought, because if the day went badly, she would be at the behest of a cab driver.

She bit her lip. "I wondered if I should have rented a car when I got here. Too late now, I suppose."

Jacob, who had been quiet until this point, suddenly spoke. "It's a wedding, right? That's where you're going?" He had obviously heard some snippets of conversation about Amelia and why she was here.

She smiled. "Yes. But not just *any* wedding," she added openly. "The wedding of my ex-fiancé."

"I see," said Jacob shooting a glance at Maia. "That's an … interesting situation." Then he smiled. "You know, I might be able to help."

Maia and Amelia both immediately looked interested.

"And just how could you help?" Maia inquired of her handsome lodger.

"Well," he said. "for starters, I have a car." He

extracted a set of keys from one of his pockets and beeped the alarm on the Mercedes rental parked in front of the farmhouse. "If you're allowed, or indeed inclined to bring a plus one…."

Maia raised her eyebrows and looked at Amelia.

"It might be rude of me to bring someone though? I don't want to mess up their seating plan…" She bit her lip.

But Jacob laughed aloud—he clearly wasn't concerned.

"A messed-up seating plan isn't nearly as terrible as inviting your ex-fiancée to your wedding. Just sayin'," he added bluntly.

This made Amelia erupt with laughter. "Do you know, you're absolutely right. To hell with their seating plan."

"That's the spirit. Every wedding needs a crasher," Jacob grinned. "What time should I be ready?"

Amelia provided him instructions and looked cheerier than she had since her arrival.

"This is going to be fun. But Jacob, just so you know, this isn't a … date, or anything OK?"

Maia smiled and said nothing while he

raised his eyebrows mischievously. "If you say so."

"No, I mean it," Amelia insisted. "I've seen the way Camilla looks at you. And in the name of solidarity and sisterhood, I wouldn't dream of stepping on her toes."

Jacob appeared thoughtful, as if he hadn't noticed Camilla's attention and was just now putting the pieces together.

"Right, got it. Not a date. And Camilla, huh?" He smiled. "Well, that *is* interesting…"

CHAPTER 15

Maia found herself with a quiet house that evening.

After some gratuitous flirting with Camilla, Jacob left with Amelia for the wedding in Positano, and Maia felt accomplished knowing that two of her guest's evenings were accounted for.

She felt gratified knowing that Amelia had some very handsome backup in confident and handsome Jacob—a fact she was sure would not be lost on her ex-fiancé.

She hoped that the younger girl got through the evening unscathed, and maybe even had a little fun.

Maia had not yet seen Hal and Lori return from their outing, and assumed that the two were having a good time and enjoying each other's company. At least she *hoped* that was what was happening.

However, with a silent house, Maia also had little for Camilla to do—so she sent her home for an evening off. She could cook her own dinner —and she believed that a person of Camilla's age needed to get out and kick up her heels every now and then, especially during the Italian summertime. This was the kind of weather to drink prosecco, dance, laugh, and fall in love.

Sighing, Maia walked toward the cliff side. The dark indigo waters of the Bay sparkled in the moonlight. Way down the coast, someone set off a firework—and the explosion boomed in the distance.

She looked in the direction of the sound down the shore towards where the wedding was being held—and saw a tiny sprinkle of light like wishes from a fairy's wand, fall toward the water.

"What a perfect night to get married," she said to the air, thinking of her own wedding. It was true that she often communed with Jim in this spot, but for a moment, she wondered if she would ever have the chance to fall in love again, get married.

"It seems hard to fathom," she said quietly. "But I know you would approve." She smiled to the sky. "Thanks for encouraging me to do this. I think I might be enjoying myself."

At that moment, Maia heard some noise from behind where she stood. She turned around to see Lori and Hal pushing the bikes they had borrowed back up the hill, headed in her direction. The gravel of the road crunched under the tires and Maia knew for a fact that it was easier going down than it was coming up. However, the pair looked happily flushed, which made her feel pleased. Lori called a greeting.

"This hill, it's a bit steep," Lori laughed.

Maia went to meet the pair. "Here, let me help you. You both must be exhausted. You've been gone all day. I trust you had fun?"

Lori was glowing like a new bride. "It was… how do I put this?" She grinned heartily. "An *incredible* day. Just wonderful. Feels like we covered the entire heel on these bikes," she said, referencing Italy's shape on the map. "I just don't think you can have the same experience in a car."

Maia glanced at Hal. The look of worry that had lined his face earlier that day was gone—and in its place was a kiss from the sun and a smile.

"Thanks for letting us take these." He motioned to the bikes as he handed Maia the picnic basket they had borrowed earlier in the day. "Lori's right—having these at our disposal, we saw so much, and when we wanted to stop and have a glass of wine or explore, we did. Thank you for, um, encouraging me...*us*," he smiled as Lori nudged him with her hip. "It was a nice break from the norm."

Parking the bikes nearby, Maia immediately went into hostess mode. "Well, I'm sure you two must be hungry. Here, let me get something going for you..."

But Lori put her hand up. "No, you relax. You've done so much for us since we arrived," she said, and Maia got the distinct impression that Lori was referring to more than simply providing a place to stay and food to eat. "We actually accumulated lots of stuff throughout the day. Some wine, cheese, other little treats;

we thought that maybe we'd come back here and share it with everyone."

Feeling touched by the gesture, Maia murmured her thanks. "That's great. Yes, please. Although, I'm all alone at the moment actually. Amelia went off to her wedding, and Jacob offered to be her escort. With Camilla's blessing of sorts." Lori raised her eyebrows, and her husband looked at her inquisitively.

"I'll tell you later," Lori smiled, wrapping an arm around Hal's waist. "Well then Maia, you chill out here. I'll get you some wine, and Hal will get everything set up inside. You relax."

Maia was about to protest, but then she gave in to Lori's request. The couple went into the house wrapped in each other's arms like besotted teenagers, with their bag of Italian goodies in tow.

Maia sat down after she watched a light turn on in the kitchen.

"Maybe I will just relax for a second," she sighed, feeling all at once appreciated and blissfully happy that her guests didn't seem to be just lodgers, but were gradually turning into friends.

CHAPTER 16

"Are you sure you're OK?" Amelia asked Jacob as she parked the car in front of the farmhouse. She stole a glance at her watch - almost three in the morning.

She hoped Maia hadn't stayed up to wait for them. She had no idea that they would be out this late. She also hadn't realised that *she* would be the one driving them home.

Amelia turned in her seat again to look at Jacob. He was a bit slumped over, but it wasn't from drinking too much—that's not why she was driving. Their night had taken an unexpected turn.

She was proud of herself—she had successfully made it through Aaron's wedding. Had wished him well, had even complimented his bride and had smugly introduced Jacob to everyone she met.

Jacob, for his part, had been the perfect date.

He had flirted with her, had pulled out her chair, escorted her gallantly on his arm and had danced with her. He had made her the envy of every woman at the party—and Amelia couldn't help but feel pleased when she saw Aaron's new wife nudge him in the ribs with a scowl, as Jacob artfully dipped her on the dance floor and returning Amelia to her seat, planted a kiss on her hand before placing a glass of champagne in it.

But then, around eleven o'clock, Jacob had received a phone call from his sister. She thought that he needed to get to the hospital, right away. It was time.

Jacob had offered to drop her back before going on to Naples, but Amelia insisted on going with him.

After all, he had been there for her—the least she could do now was be there for him.

So they had said their goodbyes and left the wedding celebration. Amelia realised as they were pulling away that it was likely she would never lay eyes on Aaron again—and it dawned on her that it was okay, that *she* was fine with that.

That the goodbye she had just uttered had been final—and the good luck that she wished to the newlyweds had been genuine.

All in all, she knew that she would be fine, better than fine actually—she was going to be *great*.

But first, she had to help Jacob—she had gathered that he wasn't fond of his father, but she also instinctually knew that he was experiencing some sort of internal crisis.

They had made it to the hospital in Naples just in time. Jacob had been stoic. He'd greeted his sister, introduced Amelia and issued an abbreviated hello to what appeared to be his extended family.

Then he had asked his sister if he could have a few minutes alone with their father. Within twenty minutes or so he returned, and she saw that his eyes were red, though she wasn't sure if it was because he had shed tears, or if he was simply tired.

Regardless, he looked emotionally spent. He

sat down next to her and she patted his hand, trying to comfort him.

Within the hour Jacob's father died.

Family members who had been with him at the time were visibly emotional. Jacob's sister Adriana approached and asked him to come with her. But he declined.

"I said what I need to," he told her, not unkindly. "I think Amelia and I are going to go now."

Then they took their leave and headed back to Villa Azalea.

Now back in the car, she asked the question again.

"We're here, Jacob. Are you okay? Let's get you out of here and get you to bed. You need to sleep."

She exited the car and headed around to his side, opening the passenger door, and wondering how she was going to get him out and into the house.

"You're going to have to help me," she smiled sympathetically. "You look like you weigh a ton of bricks."

Jacob shook his head and sighed. "Sorry, I zoned out." He hoisted himself from the car and Amelia put her arm around his waist, helping to guide him toward the house.

"Lean on me. I don't mind," she said, giving him a squeeze. "You let me lean on you earlier—I can return the favour."

Jacob put an arm around his new friend, and it was then in the darkness that she heard a choked sob.

She pretended not to. She didn't know what had happened in that hospital room—but whatever it was, she knew that the man beside her had changed in some way.

Like her, he had uttered a very important goodbye tonight, and deep down Amelia also knew that just like her, Jacob would be okay.

CHAPTER 17

"I really think we should dine al fresco and enjoy this beautiful weather. After all, how many chances do you get to eat alongside wonderful people, and with a view of Mt. Vesuvius and over the Bay of Naples?" Lori giggled as Camilla carefully instructed Amelia in the fine art of making fresh pasta.

"I couldn't agree more," said Hal, wrapping his arms around his wife and nuzzling her neck. "But I think we need a table."

He cast a glance toward the open courtyard —it was true that they had plenty of chairs, they just needed somewhere to put the food.

"Actually…" Maia said, remembering a table

they had stowed away outside the farmhouse when she and Jim had first moved in. It was made of weather-beaten wood, and Maia had wanted to dispose of it—but Jim said that it was nothing that a coat of varnish wouldn't be able to fix.

But he had never got around to it, and Maia had barely given the table a second thought —until now.

She showed Jacob and Hal where it was, and they agreed to move it to the courtyard so they could all eat outside. Within minutes, the two men had been able to create a makeshift dining room outside.

Hal went back inside to rejoin his wife in the kitchen with the rest of the group. Maia turned to follow him, but was waylaid when Jacob called her name.

"Maia, do you have a minute?" the handsome New Yorker asked. He looked tired—she knew that he and Amelia had been out late the night before. She also knew that they had ended their night at the hospital. But up until this point, she hadn't a chance to speak with Jacob about what had happened.

"Of course," she responded, halting in her path.

The young man ran a nervous hand through his hair and then smiled. "So, I just wanted to say thank you."

Smiling, she tilted her head. "For what?"

Jacob straightened his shoulders. "I took your advice, and you were right. I had a chance to talk to my father last night—before...and well, I told him that I forgave him. For everything."

"And he was ... aware of what you were saying?" Maia asked, wondering if the man had been conscious.

Jacob nodded. "He was. He was lucid—I think he knew it was the end. He was holding out to say goodbye to everyone. Me, included. But I'm glad I did it. I'm glad I didn't hold a grudge. I'm free of those feelings, and it's because of you. I don't know if I would have done that without your encouragement. I can be a bit stubborn."

Maia smiled. "Probably the Italian in you."

"Probably."

She shifted her weight from one foot to the other.

"So what's next for you? Are you going to stay on for the funeral?"

"I am," Jacob nodded. "And that's actually what I wanted to talk to you about. I was thinking of staying a little longer after that too. I thought maybe I would help my sister with some stuff, you know, settling things. And I thought I might stay and get to know some of my step-siblings. I have another brother, two sisters, maybe we have something in common, outside of sharing the same father. I figured I have vacation time that I never use, so…"

"Well, that's great. So do you plan to go to Naples and stay with them?"

He smiled bashfully. "Actually, I was hoping I could extend my reservation around here—for a bit. If that's okay of course, I don't want to intrude. But I am also happy to help out. I mean, I know you've been doing things on your own, trying to get this place in order. And you've done a hell of a job, but I don't mind helping if you could use another set of hands. I was thinking too that if I did that, then I could ask Camilla out, maybe get to know her properly."

Maia laughed. "I think that's an excellent

idea. You are most welcome, Jacob. I would love it if you stayed on here for a bit."

He looked relieved, as if he had been unsure what Maia's response would be.

"And just for the record—I'd be happy to give you any other advice you need—about this place," he added. "I don't want to toot my own horn, but let's just say that I know a thing or two about how to make money off an investment. You want to turn Villa Azalea into a proper business? I can help."

CHAPTER 18

As they all settled down to dinner beneath the stars, Hal and Lori then shared their plans about where they were going to go next.

They had decided to extend their stay in Italy too, because they were having so much fun. But better yet, and much to Lori's delight, it was Hal who suggested they head to Venice for a few days later in the week, just to "check it out."

"I'm impressed," Maia laughed. "How very *spontaneous* of you."

Hal grinned and wrapped an arm around his wife, pulling her closer. "I suppose living in the moment is a bit like riding a bike; you might not do it for a while, but the moment that you decide to, you realise that you haven't forgotten how."

"And of course Maia, please know that we are going to write an absolutely *wonderful* review on TripAdvisor. You have a gem of a place here, and I think everyone needs to know about it," Lori said, raising her glass. "Cheers to Maia. Come on everyone," she encouraged. "I cannot thank you enough for opening up your home to us. You are a wonderful hostess. And I hope that you will also allow me to call you my friend."

Maia felt her eyes become misty as the rest of the group raised their wine glasses and toasted in her honour.

Embarrassed, though grateful for Lori's kind words—she looked to try to take the spotlight off herself and turned to Amelia.

"And you, sweetheart? What's next for you?"

The young blonde smiled and shrugged her shoulders.

"I don't know. I suppose we'll see. Head back to England. I think I've been just … existing for too long, and not truly living. I need to reconnect with some friends, go dancing, drink champagne, laugh, travel, be young. I realised that last night, with Jacob's help …" she looked at her new friend and winked, "… that I'm going to be great—single or otherwise. No one is going to be in charge of my happiness except me—I'm doing what you told me, Maia. The key is back in my own pocket."

THE NEXT DAY, after Lori and Hal had departed for Venice and Jacob left with Amelia to drive her to the airport, Camilla and Maia sat in the kitchen—falling back into their old routine.

"So are you excited that Jacob is going to stay on a while?" Maia smiled, as she opened her laptop, realising that she hadn't checked her email in days.

Camilla looked over her shoulder from where she stood at the counter, slicing lemons.

"What do you think?" she replied a sparkle in her eyes.

"I think Jacob has no idea what he's getting into," Maia laughed at the same moment her email pinged with a new message. "Oh a notification from TripAdvisor. We got our first review!" she said gleefully, knowing it must be from Lori and Hal.

Clicking on the link, she accessed the website and within seconds, was reading Lori's carefully worded, and incredibly complimentary review.

"My husband and I stayed at beautiful Villa Azalea, and I cannot rave enough about this wonderful spot. Set in an idyllic location, right above the Bay of Naples, you will not find a more beautiful private residence in Italy. You wake every morning to the fragrance of lemons and azaleas, you go to bed at night under the bright stars of the Neapolitan sky and the location provides you the ultimate opportunity to explore and delight in the countryside—something you would never get staying at a big hotel. However, what makes this spot even more wonderful is Maia, the 'hostess with the mostest' who does all in her power to not only make her guests feel welcome, but like they are a member of the family. In the few days that we spent there, Maia became our friend, and I wouldn't hesitate to go back, just to see her. If you are a considering a stay in Sorrento, this is the place to be."

Maia felt a tear escape her left eye as she finished reading Lori's words. She wiped it away quickly, but Camilla had seen. "What?" she frowned. "What does it say?"

Maia duly turned the laptop around and pushed it toward her friend, who bent down to read the words on the screen. When she was finished, she gave a huge smile.

"So, that's a great review! And it's just our first. I think this will be good for business. What do you think?"

But right then, Maia's thoughts were back with her beloved, Jim.

Seems this truly is what I'm supposed to do, honey. And I think I'm going to be doing it for a very long time ...

READ on for a short excerpt of another Melissa Hill summer tale, **Days of Summer.**

DAYS OF SUMMER

EXCERPT

CHAPTER 1

Like a wheel of fortune that had last stopped in the depths of winter, the weather had since spun again and laid to rest at where summer sunshine bathed the Irish countryside.

Ella Harris looked up at the clear blue skies and smiled.

It was early June, and today the sun had some real warmth to it for the first time. With days of summer came a lifting of the spirits and a feeling of general optimism.

In her sixty-odd years she had learned to appreciate all seasons, but summer was without doubt her favourite time of the year.

"Isn't it glorious?" she said to Nina, her friend and part-time waitress in the cafe Ella

CHAPTER 1

ran in Lakeview, a beloved Irish tourist destination.

Twenty minutes-drive from Dublin City, the town was centred round a broad oxbow lake from which it took its name.

The lake, surrounded by low-hanging beech and willow trees, wound its way around the centre and a small humpback stone bridge joined all sides of the township together.

The cobbled streets and ornate lanterns on Main Street, plus the beautiful one-hundred-year-old artisan cottages decorated with hanging floral baskets, had resulted in heritage status designation by the Irish Tourist Board, and the chocolate-box look and feel was intentionally well preserved.

Ella's café was situated in a small two-storey building with an enviable position right at the edge of the lake and on the corner where Main Street began.

Early in their marriage, she and her husband Gregory took over the running of the café from her father-in-law, and Ella had spent nearly every waking moment since then ensuring that his legacy—and that of her dearly

CHAPTER 1

departed husband—lived on through good food, hot coffee and warm conversation.

"Bliss," Nina agreed wistfully. "I adore summer. No more school runs and trying to rush little Patrick out the door in the mornings,' she said fondly, referring to her five year old son.

Ella smiled, thinking not for the first time that the younger woman was doing a wonderful job of bringing up her little boy alone.

Though she knew Nina had some help from her father - after whom her son was named - being a single mum in a small Irish community wasn't an easy prospect, and she was glad that Nina had overcome her initial indecision about whether Lakeview was the best place to be, as opposed to the city where her mother resided.

Ella was also glad that a few hours a day working at the cafe at busier times helped provide a little extra income for Nina, as well as the opportunity to get out and about. Summer was one of those times.

For Ella, there was no question that Lakeview was the best place to be, but that was easy for her to say. She'd enjoyed a very happy life

CHAPTER 1

here, raised three wonderful children with Gregory and despite burying her husband almost a decade ago had even recently managed to find love again.

She smiled as she thought of the new man in her life - fellow Lakeview native Joseph - and what a whirlwind the last six months had been.

Now, the two women systematically opened each of the ten parasols providing shade for the outdoor seating area overlooking the park by the lake.

Set up for the summer season, the terrace boasted comfortable bistro chairs and tables, plus pretty red and white striped parasols. The cafe's al fresco dining area was now well and truly ready for summer and the town's habitual influx of tourists.

Ella picked up her cleaning bucket and put it next to Nina's before returning inside the cafe through the side door.

As always, the interior felt immediately warm and inviting, with delicious scents emanating from the kitchen.

She stopped to survey the space. The decor hadn't changed much over the years — it was still a warm cosy room with parquet oak flooring, shelves full of dried flowers and old country-style knick-knacks, along with haphazard seating and mismatched tables, one of which was an antique Singer sewing table.

In front of the kitchen and serving area was a long granite countertop, where any solo customers typically nursed coffees and pastries atop a row of stools.

Alongside this was a glass display case filled with a selection of freshly baked goods; muffins, doughnuts, carrot cake, brownies and cream puffs for the sweet-toothed, as well as pies, sausage rolls and Italian breads for the more savoury-orientated.

From early morning the cafe was flooded with families, friends and neighbours, all there to grab a bite to eat—and to gossip.

Ella thrived on the buzz and commotion, and the community embraced her in turn: she had become a bit of a town figurehead and confidant to anyone who came in looking for some conversation with their coffee.

The walls were adorned with watercolours by popular Dublin artist Myra Smith, who routinely spent the days of summer in town

CHAPTER 1

working on her paintings, staying at one of the nearby artisan cottages - many of which were rented out to holidaymakers at this time of year.

The artist had donated a couple of paintings to the cafe as a thank you a couple of years before, and now even though she was widely famous and sought-after, Myra still popped in now and again.

This room was heavy with memories and all the people whose lives had merged there and Ella reached under her spectacles and dabbed at her eyes.

Why was she so emotional this morning?

Then she remembered that this always happened at the start of summer, before the small community swelled with visitors from near and far, changing the dynamic of both the town and the cafe.

Like every other gone by, Ella hoped that this year's days of summer would be good for Lakeview, and she looked forward to welcoming new visitors whose arrival always managed to create some drama.

"You look so thoughtful," Colm, the cafe's resident chef called out from behind the counter. He was a true gem and had been working for Ella since he was still in school.

She was the first person he'd come out to - a difficult prospect for someone in a small Irish community like this - and they were great friends.

Colm lived with his partner in one of the artisan cottages nearby, but the two men spent a lot of time travelling the world, jetting off at quieter times of the year, during which time Ella held the fort herself.

She chuckled. "Just indulging in past memories. The Heartbreak Cafe has seen its fair share of drama," she joked, referring to the cafe's popular nickname.

Colm rolled his eyes.

"Well, if the last thirty years have been like the last two or three, it must have been crazy altogether," he said, referring to recent personal and community dramas that were somehow always central to this place.

Ella walked a few steps to the front of the counter. The glass surrounding it was sparkling clean; as always Nina had done a wonderful job.

Going out front, she looked up and down

CHAPTER 1

along Main Street. Already there was a hustle and bustle that had been absent over the last few months in the lull between Christmas and early summer.

She saw Paddy Collins walking slowly down the street, his walking stick tapping the ground in front of him.

"Hello Paddy," Ella greeted with a smile. "Time to get out of hibernation?"

He chuckled, the wrinkles around his mouth creasing even deeper. "You're right there. Any chance of a warm cuppa for an ould man, and maybe an omelette while you're at it?"

"Of course. Come on in."

Ella led the way and duly went behind the counter.

"Cheese and tomato omelette please Colm, our first official customer of the summer is here."

"Our resident swallow?"

Ella nodded. "Yep, it is indeed Paddy."

"Then summer has now *officially* begun," the chef declared and retreated to the kitchen.

It was true, Ella thought as a few minutes later, she arranged the food on a

CHAPTER 1

tray, Paddy was as regular as the seasons themselves.

When autumn arrived, he retreated into his cottage and rarely ventured out. He had a daughter, Elizabeth who stayed and kept him company during the harsher winter months.

But every year without fail, when the weather changed, almost like a squirrel which had been resting underground, Paddy Collins left his cottage and ventured out, and his first stop was always her cafe.

For the next few months, Ella knew he would eat breakfast at her establishment every single morning and she was only too delighted to have him.

"Is Elizabeth all right?" she asked, placing the tray in front of Paddy. He had chosen the same table he always did, next to the front widow where he could watched people passing by on the street outside.

"Oh she's grand, gone up north for a while," he told her.

"Shame that she doesn't spend summer here with us too," Ella commented.

"Ah, I've tried to talk to her but she'll hear nothing of it. Says this place holds too many

CHAPTER 1

memories," Paddy said, cutting up his omelette in a painstakingly slow way.

Ella knew why his daughter avoided being in Lakeview at this time of year.

One summer very many years ago, a handsome tourist had come into town and he and Elizabeth had fallen deeply in love. The young couple had spent the summer together, and when it was over, the tourist proposed and they went on to make plans for their future.

The wedding was planned for the following spring, and it was to be the wedding of the year.

Elizabeth's new fiancé returned to Dublin, supposedly to sort out his affairs, but never returned. Paddy's daughter was crushed. She had never truly moved on from that experience, viewing all men as the enemy.

"Maybe one day, she'll find someone else, and get over all that," Ella mused.

"Sure there's nothing I or anybody else can do for her," Paddy muttered, evidently eager to get on with his breakfast.

After that, the café got busy with regulars coming in for breakfast, or midmorning coffee.

Around midday, when there was a typical

CHAPTER 1

lull in activity before the lunchtime crowd, a handsome stranger walked in, standing uncertainly in the middle of the room as he scanned the bakery counter.

And here we go, Ella noted smiling, *our first summer visitor.*

DAYS OF SUMMER is available now in print and ebook.

ABOUT THE AUTHOR

International #1 and USA Today bestselling author Melissa Hill lives in County Wicklow, Ireland.

Her page-turning emotional stories of family, friendship and romance have been translated into 25 different languages and are regular chart-toppers internationally.

A Reese Witherspoon x Hello Sunshine adaptation of her worldwide bestseller SOMETHING FROM TIFFANY'S is airing now on Amazon Prime Video worldwide.

THE CHARM BRACELET aired in 2020 as a holiday movie 'A Little Christmas Charm'. A GIFT TO REMEMBER (and a sequel) was also adapted for screen by Crown Media and multiple other titles by Melissa are currently in development for film and TV.

www.melissahill.info

Printed in Great Britain
by Amazon